A SPICY NOVELLA

RHIANNA BURWELL

Copyright © 2024 Rhianna Burwell

All rights reserved

The characters and events portrayed in this book are fictitious. Any similarity to real persons, living or dead, is coincidental and not intended by the author.

No part of this book may be reproduced, or stored in a retrieval system, or transmitted in any form or by any means, electronic, mechanical, photocopying, recording, or otherwise, without express written permission of the publisher.

Content Warning

The main plot of this book is Kendall getting strapped into a glory hole and being fucked by strangers while her husband watches. It's 90% spice with very little romance, and there are non-con elements within. If these are themes you aren't comfortable with, this may not be the book for you. Take care of your mental health first, that's what matters.

Chapter 1

Kendall

"Oh my god, did you hear what happened with Natalie and Henry?" my best friend Sasha asks, the glass of wine in her hand sloshing as she speaks, her entire body swaying in front of me. She has always done that when she's a little too drunk, gotten a little too loose when her limbs. It's something that used to annoy me, but now that I don't have a white couch, I just find it endearing.

"No? What happened?" I ask, my interest piqued. Sasha always has all the drama in the neighborhood. She always knows exactly what is going on, everyone trusting her with their secrets and it's with good reason. I've never met someone as trustworthy as Sasha. She has never been one to spread gossip, or air someone's dirty laundry, at least until it comes to me.

Our newest favorite thing is to sit with a bottle of wine on Friday nights and talk about the neighbors. It's called bonding.

"So you heard about that new place opening in Roseville?" she asks, her eyes wide as she speaks, telling me everything I need to know. This is going to be a juicy story. I settle a little closer to her, wanting every detail.

"No?" I ask, on the literal edge of my seat.

"Oh my god, you need to keep up," she chides, looking at me with shock. I giggle, suddenly aware of how drunk I am. "There's this like sex club opening up in Roseville, but it's like rentable," she says, and I cock my head to the side, looking at her, trying to understand through my drunk haze what the fuck she is saying.

"A rentable sex club? What the fuck does that mean?" I ask, not understanding. Isn't the whole point of a sex club that you can go there and have sex? Or see people having sex? Now that I think about it, I'm not even sure if I know what the point of a normal sex club is.

"I guess they have like rooms that you can rent out, and do nasty group play and stuff. Anyway," she exclaims, finally getting to the good stuff. "Natalie and Henry went there last week, I guess. They have a bar and a stage for strippers and stuff. So I guess they were sitting by the bar, watching the strippers together, as like a cute couples thing," she explains, both of us making faces at each other, our eyebrows raised like there's more to the story there.

"Are we sure Henry didn't just want to see the strippers with his wife's permission?" I ask, not fully believing this. Natalie has always been a bit gullible, and it doesn't sound like something Henry would do. He is the shyest man on the block. Although it does seem like something a man would do, so maybe I'm giving him too much credit.

"That's what I said," Sasha says, leaning back, a smirk on her face as if she knows this next bit is going to excite me. "Then, guess what he did? Fingered Natalie while they sat at the bar!" she says, her eyes wide, a smile on her lips like she can't believe it.

"Henry?" I exclaim, not fully believing it either. He is the normal white picket fence kind of guy. He BBQs on the weekends and walks their dog every morning. I always imagined that he was the kind of guy to have normal, safe missionary sex, so something like this seems so unlike him, unlike the image I have of him inside of my head.

"Yes! Mr. irons-his-jeans, Henry," she says, and we both giggle. We love Henry, love most of our neighbors, actually, but we have little nicknames for most of them, enjoying making fun of them when it's only the two of us. It's all in good fun. "He got down and dirty in public with her," she says, both of us in a fit of shock and giggles.

"Okay, so I have to know, are they going to rent a room?" I ask curiously, the idea of a place so close, of a sex club just a town over, makes my blood run hot.

My husband and I have always had a normal sex life, nothing too insane. We married young when neither of us seemed to know the kinkier side of the world, and he was always just happy if I fucked him, never wanting anything more than me. It's sweet and makes me feel loved beyond belief, but honestly, the older I've gotten, the more I want some of that excitement and fun. I want to start to explore things together again as a couple.

"I doubt it. I think they just went to check it out and see what all the fuss is about. I'm shocked you haven't heard about it. I feel like everyone has been talking about it," she says, and I take a sip of my wine, enjoying our time together. The reason I haven't heard about it is because I don't hang out with the rest of the people on our block like she does. Sasha is so social, getting along with everyone, and I've never been like that. I'm not shy, not scared to talk to strangers, most of the time, but honestly, I like to be alone, like to spend long nights with my husband in our house. I like to read, and he likes to watch sports, both of us enjoy being around each other in comfortable silence. That is where I feel safe, where I feel secure, and so we tend to keep to ourselves.

Sasha and I finish talking, finishing our bottle of wine in the process. Sasha hugs me as she heads toward the door. She promises that she will be back, will come over again and drink more of my wine, and I know she will. We have been friends since I moved here, and I'm grateful for her. She makes me get out of my shell and forces me out of my cute little comfort zone. Sometimes, I need that.

I shut the door with a click and put my back against it, our conversation still ringing through my head, not leaving. I think it through, go over every word that was said again, my nerves ringing with curiosity, with desire.

I take just a second of hesitation and then grab my phone from my back pocket, moving toward the couch and searching for the place she mentioned. She didn't give me a name, but when I search "sex clubs near me" a bunch pop up. I browse for a little while, looking for clues, passing by the obvious strip joints, trying to find something specific.

One location has a new review, and it says, "this place just opened up and it's fucking sick. You can rent out rooms and do practically whatever you want in them. You have to sign about a hundred papers, but after that, let the fun begin." I read it again, slowly, knowing that this must be the place that she was talking about.

Cloud Nine

It looks just like any other bar; nothing interesting about it, but it comes up under sex clubs, so I wonder if they are going for a discreet thing, not wanting people to know just from looking at the building. That would make sense, based on what Sasha said, that it has a bar and stuff, too, not just sex rooms.

I click on the website, my curiosity getting the better of me, wanting every bit of information I can get. The website seems pretty normal, with its menu and hours lining the front page. The colors are sexy, red and black filling my phone screen, but nothing screams sex club right off the bat. But then, I click on their about us section, and a pop-up window invades my screen, asking if I'm eighteen years old and forcing me to click the box if I want to continue. I do, a little thrill going through me.

When the pop-up disappears, I see the information I have been looking for, the information that isn't hidden from the public but just a little harder to find. It describes the rooms, telling you exactly what you get when you rent one. There are ones with beds, ones with tubs, and ones with sex swings. Then, one of the rooms catches my eye: a picture showcasing what a specific room looks like, and this one makes my skin turn hot.

I watch as my fantasies come to life. I've watched porn on these kinds of things, places where men can go and fuck women, just their pussy and legs hanging out, the rest of their bodies hidden. Their legs are always strapped up in little cuffs, chained to the wall, and I feel my body react to the sight, the image of one of these contraptions sitting in front of me.

It's like a little window that you put your body through, little plastic flaps hanging down to cover you, and then you lay down, you bring your ass to the edge, and put your legs up, having someone lock you in.

The idea is that you can lay there and get fucked, used until whoever is standing on the other end, this person you don't know, is done with you. You don't know them; they don't know you. You are just a pair of legs sitting on a wall, a means to an end.

I feel my pussy throb, my entire body coming alive at the fantasy, at the idea of something like this so close.

This feels like something I shouldn't want. I'm married, happily married. I love my husband and love everything about our relationship, but I can't help but admit the idea of this, of having unknown people fuck me while I lie there and take it, does appeal to me.

I've always had a kinkier side. I love being in love. I love having one person to rely on, to snuggle with at night, to go to when things go wrong, and have come to me for comfort, too. I would never want to break up with my husband. Our sex life has always been good, always been adventurous. I think the problem... is me.

I'm just a fucking whore.

I want to be covered in cum from eight different guys. I want to be gang-banged and tied up and used until everyone is out of cum for me. I want to be traded like an object and denied orgasms until I am a writhing fucking mess. I want it all. I want to be treated like the slut that I know I am in the back of my mind.

The problem is, I don't know how to tell my husband that. I have never opened up about these things, about the nasty things I want to do, about the disgusting things I watch on my phone while I play with myself. I have no idea how he would react, if he would be open to something like that, if he would offended if I even asked. I don't know where that would put us, and that scares me.

Something about this, though, having it right here, the possibility in front of me, makes me want to find out. I've never even thought about asking my husband about these things. I have been content keeping it to myself, never giving him a clue, but now, it could be mine. It wouldn't just be an idea, something we talk about doing but never actually get around to. I could do these things, could have him with me too. We could do them together.

I feel like we could figure out a way to make these fantasies come to life, and although the idea kinda scares me, I think I may want to tell him about this and at least see what he has to say.

Chapter 2

Kendall

I listen as the door opens and closes with a small click. I wait, sitting on the couch, another bottle of wine empty next to me, alongside the one Sasha and I finished off. I didn't expect to finish another one by myself, but once I started drinking, I couldn't stop. I needed the courage because I'm not sure how I'm even going to have this conversation with him.

I'm oddly nervous. He's my husband, the person in this life I am the closest with, so I shouldn't be nervous. Yet, it feels so vulnerable. It feels so scary to open up about these things, to finally let them see the light of day. What if he doesn't understand? What if he is repulsed by me? What if he hates that I even ask, or if he is offended that I would think of such a thing? I can imagine so many ways it can go wrong, but I know if I don't at least try to trust him with this, we won't move anywhere, won't be fully open with each other, and that's an idea that I can't stomach.

"Hey...?" Nate says, taking me in, his tone changing as he looks at me, sitting on the couch, stiff, two bottles of wine on the coffee table next to me. Maybe this wasn't the best way to start this conversation, but time got away from me. I got lost in my own head, and before I knew it, I could hear his keys in the lock, and he was standing in front of me.

"Hey," I say nervously, my heart thumping in my chest. I stare at my husband as he takes off his coat, leaving him in a dress shirt and slacks, and I feel my mouth water at the sight in front of me. I have always been insanely attracted to him and enjoyed staring at every inch of his skin and his muscles. His hair is a dark brown, and I love the way it looks in my hands as I wrap myself around every piece of him, begging for more. I'm obsessed with my husband, so deeply in love that I can't believe it. I just hope he understands that I'm in love with him while also having these dirty fantasies. It doesn't take away from him. It's just... something else.

"What's going on?" he asks, turning his deep brown eyes at me, finally finished setting his stuff down. He always comes to see me first since I'm usually home before him. I start earlier and get off earlier; usually. The bank I work at opens bright and early. Today was a little different, though, because he had a meeting with a financial client for dinner to discuss this month's expenses, giving me far too much time to think, giving my mind enough time to convince myself that telling him this idea is a horrible plan.

But, even though it might backfire, I want him to know. I want him to know every thought inside of my head, no matter how scared I am for him to see them, for him to look at them up close.

"I have an idea, and I'm worried you are going to think I'm crazy," I say, my voice a wobble. The booze and the stress have gotten to me. I wanted to have this conversation with a bit more tact, not drunk on the couch, unsure how my husband was even going to react, but yet here we are. And like the angel he is, he comes to me, taking me in his arms and pulling me into his lap, instantly soothing away my anxiety, reminding me exactly who it is that I'm talking to.

We have been married for five years, together for eight, and I have yet to find a person who fits me better than he does. He is my best friend, the person I go to when anything happens to me, the person who makes me laugh the loudest, and the person I trust the most. We have had our hard times, had trouble communicating in the past, but we always seem to come together, remembering that we are against the problem, not each other. He is my safe space, and if there is anyone I can talk to about this, it's him. That is what I need to remember right now.

"What's going on?" he asks, his voice light and soothing, and he rubs circles in my back, the physical touch making me shiver.

I scooch away from him, giving us a little bit of space, and I shake myself, needing to get myself right in the head for this conversation. I push down my insecurity, and I look my husband in the eye, trying to be the goddamn adult that I know I can be.

"Okay," I start, taking a deep breath, giving myself just another moment. "This is weirdly embarrassing, and it probably shouldn't be. We have been together for so long, but we've never really talked about this," I say, knowing I'm probably not making sense, knowing that I'm probably just making him worry, but I can't seem to get the words out. They are stuck in my throat, not wanting to come out, not wanting to confess my secret to him.

"What is this about?" he asks, his eyes wide with concern, and I know I need to get this over with. I need to save my dear, sweet husband from having a heart attack right now.

"It's sexual," I say quietly, my face tinting red. I can feel the heat rise to my face, my embarrassment starting to kick in, and I do my best to push it away.

"Is this about anal? Because I've told you, I'm down for anything. I'll put my dick anywhere you want it," he says lightly, probably trying to lighten the mood, and I smile, a laugh leaking out of me. I lean toward him, placing my hand on his arm, smiling up at him, and I feel my anxiety melt. This is my husband, the one who has been by my side through everything. He wouldn't judge me or make me feel bad. We are just going to have a conversation, and if he's uncomfortable, we will just move on, no harm done. "I'm serious," he says, a smile taking over his face too.

"I know you are. That's the best part," I say with a smile. I lean back again, forcing myself to sit up and face this with courage. "Have you ever wanted to do anything extra kinky?" I ask, wanting to gauge where he is at, what his level is with these things. I've had these fantasies for years, thought about how hot it would all be. I've masturbated to the thought probably a hundred times, but I don't know if he has the same tendencies.

"Uh... I don't know..." he says, his sentence trailing off. He looks around the room for a second, thinking. I give him a moment, wanting him to answer honestly, wanting to hear exactly what is going through his mind. "Of course, I have fantasies but doesn't everyone?" he asks, looking back and me. When he looks at me, his brown eyes looking into mine, I feel safe, comforted.

"I don't know," I reply honestly. "I know that I do. I have a lot of dirty fantasies, but they have just been that, fantasies," I say and take a deep breath. "I was talking to Sasha, and she told me about this sex club, and I can't get it out of my head. I keep thinking that my fantasies could become reality, and I can't stop thinking about it or imagining how hot it would be," I say, getting carried away, rambling now. I clear my throat, trying to recenter on the conversation. "Do any of your fantasies...ever have other people involved?" I ask timidly, not knowing how to ask my question without fully asking the question. I know this would be easier if I didn't dance around it and I just came right out with it, but this feels so personal. It feels like baring my soul to him, and although I have done that before, this feels different. I want to tell him what I'm thinking, but I want him to bare his soul, too.

"Uh..." he says with a nervous chuckle. "Sometimes. Why?" he asks, and I know, at this moment. I have to be brave, have to tell him everything, because I can keep beating around this, can keep trying to get him to say it first, but he doesn't know what to say, so I need to just do it.

"Sometimes, I think about getting fucked by like a group of other guys, while you watch," I say lightly, staring at him, looking at his face for any sign of disgust or even dislike. I search for any uncomfortable feeling, but he just stares back at me, his eyebrows raised as he processes my words. He licks his lips and then says something I am not ready for in the slightest.

"Am I participating or just watching?" he asks, and I feel my own eyebrows raise, his question throwing me. I expected him to be grossed out, to hate the idea of me fucking someone else. I thought he would think of it like cheating, but instead, he wants to know more, wants details about the fantasy that I've kept closest to my chest.

"I've thought about both," I admit, the fantasy being more about me being used, about a bunch of guys fucking me while he's there. "Usually, it doesn't matter if you participate or not, but it's more like..." I hesitate, trying to put my thoughts into words correctly. "It's like you are giving me away. Like you want to share me. You are permitting all these guys to fuck me because you want them to experience my body too," I say lightly, my face heating, my body unsure how to respond. Even thinking about the fantasy makes me hot, makes my skin heat, and my pussy starts to throb but nerves are running through me too, forcing my body into a state of confusion.

Nate swears under his breath, looking away for just a second, and for just a moment, I worry he *is* disgusted with me, so grossed out by what I have described that he is turning away from me, but when he looks back at me, the only thing in his gaze, is pure lust. "You'd be into that?" he asks, his voice deep, hoarse.

I stare back at him, not really expecting this turn of events. I thought he would need more information, would need to be convinced that this is a good idea, that it could be hot. Of course, I was never going to pressure him, but I thought he would need a little push because I figured this would be too far out of his comfort zone.

"*You* would be into it?" I ask, my voice full of shock and uncertainty. I stare into my husband's eyes not believing that he would have these fantasies, too.

"I mean..." he hesitates, thinking again. I know him well enough, know he's trying to get his words in order, too. It seems we are both trying to make this digestible for the other, and that was not what I expected to happen. "I've watched porn like that before. I never really thought about actually doing it, but... I can't say I hate the idea," he says while looking at my eyes, his signal that he means precisely what he is saying.

"You'd let... another guy fuck me?" I ask, not sure if I'm understanding what he is saying. It feels too good to be true. Could our kinks line up like this? Could it be that my husband is my best friend, my partner, the best person I know, and also matches me sexually?

"When you say it like that, it sounds bad. I think for me... I think about it like you said. You are mine. No man is going to touch you unless I give them permission, but that pussy is just so fucking good, so fucking sweet, that I have to share, have to give other men a taste, so they know how good it is, but you come home with me at the end of the night," he explains, and I swear my body lights on fire right in my living room. I gulp, and I watch as his eyes track the movement, his eyebrows raising, the meaning of my actions perfectly clear.

"So you would... be into it then?" I ask, wanting him to say it, wanting him to make it clear.

"Yeah. I mean, we would need to talk about it, but I could see us doing it," he says, and I stare at him, my mind not connecting with what is happening at all. "Do you like the idea of another man fucking you?" he asks, prodding, probably just wanting to hear me say it, just wanting to tell him my fantasies.

"Yeah. I think about it a lot, how good it would feel to be filled with another man while you watch," I whisper, looking at him, my body tense, full of desire, full of need. God, this whole conversation is turning me on, making me into a puddle of mush. He knows it too, his eyes tracking me, watching me closely, and my husband is too fucking observant not to notice what a horny thing I am right now.

Nate's hands move to his dress shirt, the buttons holding his shirt together, while his eyes stare into mine. I sit there, frozen, unsure what to do, my body so fucking alive, but my mind not working. I'm so turned on, so horny. This conversation took a turn I was not ready for, and now I'm sitting here, unsure how to act. I at least had a plan in my head, knew how I could make him understand that my kink isn't cheating, that it is because of how much I love him, because of the bond that we have, that I want him to give me to other men, want to let other men fuck me. I knew how I was going to act if he was unsure, but this... this is throwing me for a total loop.

"I knew you were dirty, but this? Asking me to let another man fuck you? This is fucking filthy, Kendall," he says, undoing the last button on his shirt. He removes his white shirt in a slow, yet efficient move. My gaze travels down his stomach, moving over each inch, soaking it up with reckless abandon, not caring that he is watching me check him out. We have been married for long enough, he knows exactly how I feel about his body.

I bite my lip, unsure of how to respond, knowing how badly I want this, want him to fuck me, want him to thrust his cock inside of me, with the thought of actually fulfilling this fantasy sitting on both of our brains. I want us to role play, to pretend that it is happening.

"Is that what you want? Want another man to use this tight fucking cunt?" he asks, standing up and moving toward me, cupping my face with one hand and my pussy with his other. I stare into his eyes, and I see a level of vulnerability there, that he wants to know if this is serious. We can sit here and talk all day, but when it comes down to it, if we are actually going to do this, actually going to fulfill this fantasy that has been growing in both of us, we need to know what we are getting into.

I nod, answering his question. I want it so fucking badly. I want him to watch as other men find pleasure inside of me. I want him to watch as I drive them fucking wild, making them all come apart, making them all cum far too fucking quickly. I want him to watch as they fill me with their seed, and then, I want him to kick them all out and fuck me with it, using their cum as lube for himself, finding his own pleasure in my body.

Chapter 3

Nate

I think I am the luckiest man on this fucking planet. I swear to god, my wife was sent down from the heavens above with my name tattooed on her soul. I have never wanted another person since I first saw her. Never even wanted to make eye contact with any other woman. I knew I needed her, knew my soul was made for hers, after our first conversation. I've wanted her every day since then. I am thankful for her because without her in my life, I don't know where the fuck I would be.

I've always felt lucky, always thought I had everything I could ever need, but while I smash my lips against my wife's, with the sole intention of sticking my cock inside of her within the next five minutes, I feel even more lucky.

I've always been a kinky guy, always had sex on the brain. When I first met Kendall, we went at it daily, both of us unable to scratch the itch that was inside of us. We were insatiable for each other, starved. You could not give me enough of her. I wanted to be inside of her all hours of the day. We fucked like rabbits, constant.

We cooled down after a while, both of us figuring out that we couldn't be in that honeymoon phase forever, but I always wanted something more. I wanted to own her, to have control over her, to make her mine in a way that I couldn't even explain to myself.

The thing is, I am so fucking happy. I didn't want to be greedy. I didn't want to ask my beautiful, insanely smart, perfect wife to give me more. I didn't want to ask her for something that she wasn't openly giving to me because if she wasn't already thinking it, then it would be a big ask.

So, I said nothing, totally content without explaining this craving inside of me. I watched porn every once in a while, had fantasies in my head, and kept going on with my life, happy just to breathe the same air as Kendall. I didn't want to push my luck.

Yet, here I am, my wife asking, begging me, to let other men fuck her, to let her be used as they please, to let another man fill her with their cum, using her cunt for their own pleasure. She is asking me to own a piece of her that she has never given me, and at this moment, I fucking gotta believe that there is something spiritual going on here because I have never met someone so fucking perfect for me as Kendall.

"If you're going to act like a slut, I'm going to treat you like one," I mutter softly, my hand still cusping her cunt, holding it in my hand, owning it. I've always felt this inside of me, this ownership over her pussy, over her body, but part of me thought it was just me being a crazy ass man, wanting to own everything that I like, but this, this is different. I want to own her, want to give her body out as I please. I want her to ask before she touches herself because this cunt, it's mine.

The idea that she feels even semi-similarly, that she wants me to own her, makes my cock so fucking stiff it aches. I should relax after work. I should sit on the couch and drink a beer. I should ask my wife how her day was, ask how work treated her, ask how Sasha was because I know my wife saw her today. I should want to spend time with her, but all I can think about is slipping my cock inside of her and making her know exactly how I fucking feel. I want to act out every nasty fantasy we both have seemed to be having lately.

She looks up at me, pure lust in her gaze, a sort of obedience there, too. Her expression isn't one I have seen before. She looks at me like she knows that she is mine and is going to give me ownership over her body. I swear I'm going to cum in my fucking pants if I look at her for too long.

"Get on your knees," I say, not caring that I'm acting like a fucking teenager, not caring that we are right in front of our frosted glass front door. The whole neighborhood would watch her suck my cock. It would bring me joy actually, having them all see what she did to me.

She moves instantly, her body not even hesitating for a second. She is on her knees in front of me, unfastening my belt, looking up at me with sin in her eyes. She licks her lips, like she can't wait for the taste of me, and I swear it makes me weak. How I got so goddamn lucky is beside me. I must have been a real saint in my past life.

"Is this what you want? Want to suck my cock while another man fucks you?" I ask, watching as she pulls my pants down, her hands barely even undoing the zipper before they are at my ankles.

She nods at my words, her breathing fucking ragged. We have had good sex, amazing sex in the past, but this animal need is new for both of us. I have been obsessed with my wife for years, but this desire to be inside of her, to stay right there, to keep my cock inside of her all fucking day, just so she knows who owns her, is overwhelming. It feels like an animal has been unleashed inside of me, and now there is no getting it back, no getting back to the calm and cool husband that I used to be.

She pulls down my boxers, freeing my cock, and it bounces, hard, stiff, desperate for her to touch it, but she just stares up at me, waiting, looking to me for direction. I swear to god, I'm going to cover her entire body in my fucking cum.

"Open up," I mutter, my voice rough and needy. I need this more than I have needed anything. She looks so fucking pretty staring up at me, her tongue darting out as she opens her mouth. She listens so fucking well for me, gives me everything, and I never expected to be here with her. I never expected she would want some of the nasty things that I want.

I place my cock on her tongue, feeling the wetness against my tip, and I groan. I'm going to cum way too fast, way quicker than I want to. I want to savor this moment because it feels like a big one. It feels like the first moment I am seeing every single part of her, all of her. Even the parts she is most ashamed about, the parts she has worked to hide from me.

"Play with your cunt," I murmur as she sucks the tip of my cock into her mouth. "Pretend it is another man there, touching you," I say, and close my eyes, trying not to think about how good this feels, how badly I want to shove my cock down her tight little throat and use her. I want to own her body, but I also want to know how far I can push her.

If I'm going honest, part of me is worried that she just wants this as a fantasy. Maybe she just likes the idea of someone fucking her, of someone using her body while I watch. I want to know if she is being serious and, if she is, just how serious she is being. Is this something she just wants to talk about? Wants me to dirty talk about while I fuck her silly? Or does she actually want me to start planning this, finding men who I think should fuck my wife?

I think my answer is going to depend on how she acts tonight.

Chapter 4

Kendall

My husband stands over me, his cock slowly thrusting into my mouth, and I close my eyes, enjoying the sensation. I have always loved giving him blow jobs, letting him use my mouth. The key word there is *him*. I have never enjoyed a blow job with anyone like I do with him because he is so fucking vocal. He moans and breathes heavily and makes these faces that bring me closer and closer to orgasm even though he isn't even touching me yet.

I close my eyes and imagine what he is asking, imagine that there is a man behind me, ready to fuck me closer and closer to my husband, forcing me to take his cock to the back of my throat. I want another man here, to have his cock resting against my ass, teasing me, making me wait for it. I'm so desperate to be fucked in every single one of my holes, and I wish this fantasy would become a reality already.

"That feel good, baby?" he asks, and I open my eyes again, moaning against his shaft. I take it another inch, trying like hell not to gag. He isn't huge, isn't a footlong for anything, but he is girthy and long enough to make my throat tighten up as he gets farther and farther down. He has always made me gag, always filled my throat with his cock to the point of pain, but this time, I want to take him all, show him how amazing I am, how deserving I am of fucking other men.

I want him to tell all the other guys just how amazing I am with my mouth. I want him to brag about me and act like I'm a dog who is good at doing tricks. I want him to boast about how good I am in bed, and when they ask for more details, I want him to give them something even better.

I feel my eyes roll to the back of my head as I stroke my clit, easing pleasure out of me like a siphon. I need it. I need to cum with these thoughts in my mind. I want to cum with his cock in my throat, both of us imagining another man behind me.

I didn't think this was how tonight was going to do, didn't think that I would be on my knees moments after I confessed to my husband, but here I am as he fucks my tight throat, easing his cock in and out, pushing my head back with each stroke.

He pulls out suddenly, and I whimper with desperation, not wanting this to end yet. I want to be fucked, want to have my pussy filled, but I want more than anything to continue with this fantasy. I want to pretend that my hands are someone else's, and that only makes it better when my husband has his cock in my throat.

I complain too quickly, though, because he just shifts me toward the wall, pushing my back up against it, and then he's in my mouth again, fucking me even harder than he was before. He goes deep, so deep that I can't fucking breathe. I start to panic a little, the air not making its way to my lungs, but he pulls out, knowing my body, knowing my reactions better than I seem to know them myself.

"Relax for me," he says, bringing his hand down on my cheek and moving my hair out of the way. I watch as the loving side of him takes over in his eyes, and god, I'm so in love it isn't even fair. I want him to be with me forever. I want his voice in my head. My husband is my best friend, my everything, and I want to go through this together. I want us to trust each other because the way he is looking down at me, like I could do no wrong, like I am the apple of his eyes, makes me fucking melt.

I wouldn't be open to doing this with anyone else, but I know my husband will keep me safe and will keep me comfortable the entire time.

"Is this how you're gonna respond when another dude is fucking you? All tense and stiff? Like you don't want it?" he asks as he slides his cock back into my mouth, and I go to shake my head, but his cock is so far back in my throat that I can barely move. "Maybe they will like that even more," he mutters, before pulling out again, giving me air. "Maybe they would like the idea of forcing you, of making you take another man's cock while your husband is sitting there watching," he says with a smirk, sliding back in so slowly while I stare up at him, with nowhere to go, no escape. Still because of the trust we have and because of the way I feel for this man, I know it's going to be okay, I know he's going to take care of me, even as he uses my body in the most punishing way.

He pulls out again, and I stutter out a cough, my throat starting to ache from his intrusion. He backs up, staring at me, drool running down my fucking face, his cock leaving me probably looking like a mess, but he looks at me like I am an angel that he ordered. I sit there and stare at him, trying to catch my breath.

"Get this pussy on the couch," he growls, his voice deep as he leans down to look me in the eye. He stares at me, his eyes blazing with lust and desire, and my body listens right away. I don't have time to think, don't have time to second guess. I want this too badly. I want him inside of me.

I stand up, my body still fully clothed, while he kicks off his work pants, fully taking off every inch of his clothing, leaving him in front of me in all his glory. My husband isn't ripped. He doesn't have a six-pack but he has definition, muscles. He works out often, using the gym as his own personal stress ball, and he fucks me ruthlessly, giving himself a workout then too.

I give myself another second to look at him, giving myself one last glance, and then bring my body to the couch, laying down instantly, the soft cushion beneath my back. He moves toward the stairs, farther away from me, but I don't understand. I thought he was going to fuck me. He got me fucking lust drunk, and now what is he going to do? Leave me like this? Leave me to suffer?

He leaves the room, his body disappearing up the stairwell, and I just sit there and stare for a moment, not even knowing what to do. I want this so badly I think my panties are soaked through, but if he doesn't want to do this, if he has changed his mind, I can't fault him. I understand. What I'm asking for is a lot.

I hear his footsteps upstairs, and I bring my gaze to the ceiling, trying to track him based on his movements. He walks toward my side of my bed, the creak in the floorboards is one that I know far too well, and he opens something. I'm not sure what, though. I can't figure out what he is doing, but suddenly I hear his footsteps walking back down the stairs, coming closer, and my gaze darts back to the entrance of the living room.

He walks in, a devilish smile on his face, his hand hidden from me. I bring my head to the side, trying to see what he has, trying to see what he is holding in his hand, but it's no use.

He comes closer, his body coming within a few feet of me, and his cock is still hard, standing at attention in front of me. I lick my lips, my body lined up on the couch so that if I look sideways, my cheek against the cushion, I have a direct line of sight to his cock. It is a mouthwatering angle, and I wish he would step closer so that I could have another taste. I'm not sure if I can get enough of him.

"Are you being serious about what you want?" he asks, staring at me, completely naked. I look at him for a second, my brain not even processing what just came out of his mouth because it was the last thing I expected.

"What do you mean?" I ask, completely breathless. I don't know how he can have a conversation with his cock out like that. I don't understand how he isn't flustered, how his brain isn't going back to sex every chance it can get. I want him inside of me, in any one of my holes, so badly that my brain refuses to even work properly.

"Do you actually want to fuck another man? Or other men?" he asks, clarifying, both of us knowing that it wouldn't just be one. I don't think I would be satisfied with just a three-way. I want so many loads of cum inside of me that I can taste them all. I want to be so filled with their seed that I can't move an inch without leaking all over myself.

"Yes," I say, lifting my head up and supporting my weight on my elbows. I stare into his eyes, trying to figure out what he is getting at.

"If you want this, if you want me to watch other men fuck you, for them to use that tight little cunt, you are going to have to do better than that," he murmurs, literally looking down on me. I stare up at him, knowing that I would do anything to convince him that I'm serious. This isn't just a small fantasy. This isn't something I have thought of a few times and would like to try out. I've been thinking about this for so long, been imagining how it would go. I don't just want to do this. I crave it.

He pulls his hand out from behind his back, and what is in his hand shouldn't surprise me. I should have been able to guess this and should have known that my sex-driven husband wasn't going to walk away from stuffing me.

He holds my biggest dildo, bright pink, veins running down the shaft, even a little slit at the tip. He holds the dildo that I've taken so many times. It is the closest to looking like a real man's cock, beside the color.

I don't have a lot of dildos, just a few that I like to play with while my husband is at work, and, of course, he is holding my favorite, the one I use the most often to get myself off.

"You take this, while I fuck your throat, and when you do, I want you to imagine that it's another guy, another man with his cock inside of you, filling that tight hole up," he says, moving closer to me, his cock bouncing as he moves, his body fucking perfect.

"Yes, yes, please," I say instantly, not caring that I sound desperate. That is half of the point. I am desperate. I'm such a fucking whore that I can't even stick to one man, can't even resist the urge to let any man fuck me because that's what I'm good for.

"I'm gonna pretend too, and I'm gonna make sure it feels real. If you actually want to do this, we can't just go into willy nilly, we need to figure out if we are both going to be okay with this, and, if we are, we can book a room at the club," he says, my heart skipping a beat as his words register in my brain.

"You're serious?" I ask, my mind not believing it. I didn't even think he would be open to this, and now he wants to do it? He wants to act out this fantasy with me. "What do you get out of it?" I ask without thinking, my mind not catching up that he might find this attractive too. I have convinced myself for so long that this isn't something that any man would be okay with, that no man would want his wife to be fucked by strangers.

"The idea of you taking another guy's cock, of letting him pleasure this fucking cunt, is so hot, Kendall. How do you not understand? I want you to feel every bit of pleasure that you can, and then, at the end of the night, you come home with me. These guys only get a taste. They don't get to have you, and that's the best part. It's like letting a guy hold your trophy and then taking it back home at the end of the day and putting it in the case. You are all mine, so they can look, they can even touch, but when the time comes, when the end of the night hits, they are all going to be walking home alone, their cocks desperate for another round, but I'm going home with you. I'm gonna go home with this tight pussy, and I will use it as much as I please," he says with a smirk, his face coming closer and closer to mine, until he is just inches away, our breath mingling together. I want him so badly, want to act out exactly what he just said.

"I want that. I want to be used, want to tease all these guys until they can only think of me," I admit, my face heating as my words register. They are the full truth, the entire reason this fantasy is so fucking hot. It is degrading to be treated like an object, but for some reason, being treated like an object, in this context, makes my body zing with pleasure, with pure desperation.

"That's because you're a whore. You like teasing guys because you can't help yourself, right?" he asks, bringing the dildo to my hands and giving it to me, his head motioning for me. "Take another man's cock," he whispers, his gaze so full of desire that I could die. I want him so badly, want to do this, but more so, I want to keep this trust going with my husband. Being able to do this with him, being able to experience this with another person that I trust so deeply, is what I truly want.

I settle back on the couch, holding the dildo in my hand while I push my pants and panties down, exposing myself to the air. He looks down at my pussy, his gaze turning molten. I spread my legs, the best I can with my pants still around my ankles, and bring the dildo to the entrance of my cunt, looking up at him, wanting him to tell me what to do.

"Do it. Take his cock, baby, make yourself cum with another man's cock," he says, and so, I do.

We find pleasure in each other, him in my throat and me on my dildo. The entire night felt so good, so right, like nothing we had experienced yet.

I want more. I want to experience the real thing, together. I feel like a fire has caught inside of me, and all I want is to feel the burn. I want my soul to be burned to the ground, the pleasure taking its place. I thought when we started this that it would make me feel better and would curb this desire inside of me, but it has only stoked it, and made me want to act out my fantasy, *our* fantasy, even more.

Chapter 5

Kendall

I open my car door, my nerves running through me like lightning bolts. I didn't think this would actually happen a few weeks ago. I didn't think I would be staring at the club in front of me, watching as the lights on the sign changed colors, watching it invade my senses. I thought I would be at home snuggling with my husband, being the perfectly normal white picket fence couple that I always thought we were.

Boy, has the last few weeks changed things.

We have kept fucking, imagining what this is going to be like. For me, it has been a fun roleplay, something that has made our sex even better, but for Nate, I think he is doing it to make sure I actually want this. He always has this look about him, like he will be there to catch me if I fall, and that only makes me love him more. It makes this whole thing even better, knowing that between us, the trust is still there, even if another man's dick is inside of me.

I do appreciate him, though. I'm glad we have done it so much to make sure this is something we want. It would suck it get here, get a lot of other people involved, and then have to tell them to go home. My mind and body not yet ready for this experience.

I think that has been the hardest part, making sure I have my mind wrapped around what is going to happen. You can't consent if you aren't aware, if you aren't right here in the moment, so I've been working hard to make sure I know what I'm getting myself into and opening myself up to this experience.

"Are you sure about this?" Nate asks as he steps around the car, looking at me with lust in his gaze and just a hint of concern. I smile at him, looking him in the eyes when I answer because I know it is my job to get myself ready for this and to make sure he is ready for this, too.

"Yes, I am. As long as you are okay with this," I say, giving him a moment to back out, too. "We can just keep having filthy sex and talking about it. We don't have to do it if you don't want to," I add, needing him to know that this isn't something I need. The only thing I need in my relationship is him. If I have that, I will be fine. I just want to make sure he isn't doing this with some false sense of care, him trying to take care of me and my needs.

He smiles back at me, his hand reaching out for mine, and I take it. His hand is larger than mine, by quite a bit, and I smile as I walk beside him. "I don't want to go home, not with the idea of what is about to happen," he says, his voice a fucking purr. I try to keep my reaction to myself, not sure how much his words influence me, but I hear a snicker next to me, and I know I'm caught. "God, the guys are gonna have fun with you," he mutters, and I feel myself light on fire.

God, I was trying not to get my hopes up, trying to make sure that if he pulled back, that if he wanted to go home, there wouldn't be a hint of disappointment in my gaze, but now that we are walking closer and closer to the door, I am so fucking excited.

He opens the door for me. The outside of the building looks mostly normal. Brown brick and tinted windows. The only extravagant thing about it is the sign. It's a cloud, an ode to their namesake, Cloud Nine and is has a pastel color scheme. Pinks and blues shoot through the sky, lighting up the night life.

I would probably think it is any other bar or grill, not giving the name a second thought, and I think that is what they want. Although the information was easy to find eventually, I know half of this club's idea is to be kept more secretive. It feels a little dirty to even be walking in, both me and Nate knowing what is going to happen between these brick walls, but the rest of the world has no idea.

I step inside, him joining me seconds later, and I look around. It looks… like any strip club but nicer. It doesn't look extreme, doesn't look extra sexy. There is no real giveaway that people can fuck in private rooms. There is a bar on one wall, a decently busy bar, actually. I wonder how many people come here just to hang out, to grab a drink after work, and watch the dancers taking up the stage, which comes out of the opposite wall.

From this point of view, it just looks like a fancy strip club. It doesn't look like people act out their nastiest fantasies here or like people find insane pleasure. It looks like just any other place for men to throw money at women, for them to feel as if they have some sort of power.

We walk back, crossing the bar, to a hallway. When we made our appointment over the phone, after asking about a hundred questions, they directed us to where to go. By the bathrooms, down the single hallway in the entire building, there was a door with a big red 'X' on it. That is where we would find what we need.

We walk slowly to the door, and my nerves are suddenly higher than I expected. I tried to prep so much, to prepare myself for this moment, for being laid out on a table and fucked by so many different guys, but standing here, my body is thrumming with energy, unsure what to do with it all.

Nate turns to me, grabbing both of my hands in his own, and I smile up at him, comforted by his touch. "Are you sure about this?" he asks again, gaze moving back and forth between my eyes, trying to read my expression. "We can stop at any point, any time you are uncomfortable, any time it is too much, but once we get through those doors, it's going to start. We are going to be there, naked, and if you want to stop, it might be a lot harder," he explains, and I nod along with him, following his words.

"I want this," I whisper, putting every ounce of my energy into making him believe the truth. I want this so badly. I'm not going to get scared, not going to turn back. I want what is behind that door, and I know, if his hard cock, the one currently poking me in the belly, is any indication, he wants this too.

Chapter 6

Nate

We walk through the door together, her first, then me. It feels like something is shifting between us, and I'm sure it is. This is a big step, a big step of trust, of kink. There is a lot happening. Although I am so fucking excited, so turned on by the idea of her getting fucked by other men, I don't want anything to shift with *us*. I want to continue being the couple we always have been. But that's the biggest thing about this, trusting that even if something goes wrong, we will make it through together.

The room is not at all what I was expecting. It looks more like a lobby than anything. It seems... professional. The receptionist behind the desk, only a few feet after you walk into the door, greets us with a small smile. She lifts from her chair to shake both of our hands. I notice she is wearing a pencil skirt. I don't usually take note of women's fashion choices, but that was the last thing I was expecting.

I thought she would be in a thong or something skimpy, something that someone who works at a sex club would wear. Instead, she gives the aura that we just walked into a bank and should keep our voices down.

"I'm Noami, and you must be... Kendall and Nate, right?" she asks, glancing down at a sheet on her desk. We nod and agree and she motions for us to sit in the lobby area. Every wall is filled with chairs, lining the square-shaped room. It's set up as if many people frequent the space, which seems unlikely, given the business, but who am I to say?

"Have you ever been here before?" she asks, looking between the both of us, her gaze entirely professional. She sits a few seats away, a clipboard in her hand, ready to take notes.

This entire thing is throwing me off kilter. Beyond this door, there is a strip club, women dancing on a stage while men watch. In the opposite direction, there are rentable rooms to fuck. This feels like a weird middle ground like we entered into a whole different dimension when we entered through that door, and we will go back once we enter through another.

We both shake our heads, uncertainty thrumming through the room, our energy changing.

"Okay, so this may feel a bit formal," she says with a small smile, and I nod instantly. She laughs lightly, and my wife smiles at me, both of us showing our nerves on our faces. "At the end of the day, this is a business. We have to keep everything legitimate. We aren't in the business of getting shut down, so this part is the not-so-fun part. We have to make sure you both consent to what is about to happen. We recommend couples choose a safe word, just in case, and I'm going to make you sign so many papers that your hands start to bleed," she says, her smile still staying put. She is making this entire experience more comfortable, making my anxiety wash away.

I glance at my wife, and she smiles at me. I give her a questioning look, wondering if she is up for this, if she wants to continue. She nods, looking at me like she might laugh. I'm glad she finds it humorous that I keep asking, but I can't help myself. It feels surreal that we are here, that she is open to this, and I just need to make sure she wants this as badly as I do.

We went through the whole process with Naomi, which honestly wasn't as bad as she made it seem. We chose the safe word 'grapefruit,' and we both had to explain what it was that we thought was going to be happening in that room, just so she knew we were on the same page, so she knew we were both fully consenting to this. Other than a slight awkwardness, it went off without a hitch.

"The good news is that after this, if you decide you want to come back, you don't have to do this every time. The papers have been signed, and they are good for a year. We ask that you describe each scene you want when you enter, just in case something changes, but at the end of the day, next time, this should be a whole lot easier," she says, and me and my wife both nod at her, soaking in the information.

"So, next order of business, when did you tell the other guys to come?" she asks, looking between the two of us. My wife looks at me, a question in her gaze, like she doesn't know the answer to this question, and she doesn't. This was my job of the night, to set up men who would fuck her, strangers that she didn't know. That is half of the appeal. She doesn't know these guys and won't even know who is on the other side of the wall. She is about to be fucked by complete strangers.

"I told them six-thirty," I say, glancing at my watch, seeing that we still have fifteen minutes until they are supposed to arrive.

"Okay, perfect. I'm going to give you some time to go into the room and get settled. There is a light above the platform that will be red when you enter, and when the scene starts and I have let the guys into the other room, it will go green. Just so you know. I'm sure you will hear them too, but that is your sign that they are entering," she explains, and we both nod again. My anticipation is starting to run under my skin, making me jumpy. I'm glad she is taking this seriously, glad she is covering everything, making sure this is a safe experience for everyone, but I'm ready to be in the room, ready to help my wife get set up, get naked, ready to be fucked.

I'm doing my best to keep my body in check, not wanting to get a boner while this stranger of a woman is in front of us, but it's fucking hard with my wife next to me, the thoughts of what is about to happen so clearly in my head.

"Okay, go ahead and head into door number three, down the hall, to the right. You are entering into the room with the glory hole, where you will be laying," she says, looking at my wife. "There will be another door connected to the room that leads into the other side, where the other guys will be. It only opens from your way, so they can't open it, but you can. It's your choice if you want to, but just for your safety, we made sure it doesn't even have a doorknob on their side," she says, and the motions for the first hallway, closest to the door we entered.

We both get up, gather our things, and walk down the hallway. I don't know why I'm so nervous, why I feel like I could jump out of my skin. I feel like I'm going to throw up and cum at the same time, which is a wild-ass feeling.

We open the door with the big, bold 'three' and when the door swings open, my every fucking fantasy comes alive in front of me. We enter and close the door, giving us just a minute to breathe before this starts.

I look over at my wife, her deep brown hair and her golden brown eyes. I pull her body against mine, loving the feel of her body against mine.

"You're gonna get fucked right there," I say, motioning to the contraption that is against the far wall. It almost looks like a bed, half of it inside this room, half inside the connected room. It has an opening, for her body to sit, and little plastic flaps to keep her body hidden from the people on the other side.

"I'm kind of nervous," she says, a giddiness to her voice. I smile down at her and then bring my lips to hers. She is the calm in my storm, always, and I'm far too excited for this, far too excited to see her cum on another man's cock, so I use her to ground me, to bring me right back down to earth.

I slide my hands under her shirt as I slip my tongue in her mouth, enjoying the familiar feeling, the familiar taste of her.

I lift her shirt above her head, lifting it off of her and throwing it against the wall, not caring, needing her to be undressed as soon as humanly possible.

She is breathing heavily Her chest heaves with every lungful of air, and I unhook her bra quickly, needing to see her tits, needing to see her bare against me. I don't want to wait any longer, don't want to push this off when we are here, in the room we have been thinking about for weeks.

She is so fucking sexy, and when her bra slips down, hitting the floor, I swear I almost start drooling at the sight of her bare tits in front of me. I bring my mouth down, not caring that we should be getting ready, not caring that we have less than ten minutes until the next room is going to be filled with other guys who want to stick it inside of my wife. I need her, need to feel her body against mine, need the constant comfort that I have had for years now.

I suck her nipples into my mouth, swirling my tongue around, just in the way that I know she likes. She moans for me, her back arching lightly, silently begging me to give her more. I run my hands up and down her side until I feel goosebumps. I cup her tits in my hands, feeling the weight of them, feeling her soft skin. I pull away, looking her in the eyes while I pinch her nipples between my fingers.

"I'm already so wet," she says, looking down at her chest, watching my movements, watching as I squeeze her tits in my hands, content just with the feel of her.

"For me? Or for them?" I ask. I watch as her cheeks heat. I like embarrassing her, making it known that her desire for other men's attention isn't lost on me. I see through her so clearly, and she knows it.

"Both," she whispers, her voice hoarse. I lean down again, kissing her chest, needing her skin against my mouth, and then I go lower, until I'm on my knees, kissing her belly, loving the way it flexes as I hit a ticklish spot. She breathes in and out as I make my descent, and then I slowly peel her leggings off, taking her thong with it in one fell swoop.

I need her naked. I need to see her beautiful body in front of me. I need to see what all these other guys are going to see, but only for a night. That is the best part. I don't mind sharing, giving them a small taste, but at the end, she is coming home with me, fucking me in my bed. They only get her for a night, but I get her forever.

She kicks off her shoes and then socks, stepping out of her pants, and leaving her fully exposed in front of me. I know I should stand, know we should get situated before anyone else comes into the other room, but I want just another minute with her body, want to use it to ground myself.

I run my hands up her thighs, and she just stares down at me, a pout in her gaze. She wants more, and I know she does. She has always been a needy little thing in bed, never able to be satisfied with just one orgasm. She is constantly seeking more, wanting more pleasure. She does the same right now, begging me with her eyes to touch her, to make her cum before another man sets foot in the room next door.

There will be a handful of men walking through that door any second, and she still wants me to pleasure her first. God, she is insatiable.

I bring my hands up, up, up, wanting to tease her, wanting her to whimper my name while they are on the other side jerking their cocks, but I get carried away, losing my self-control. I can't help but want to touch her, wanting to feel her skin against mine, wanting to feel if she is being truthful or not about how wet she is.

I bring the tips of my fingers to the apex of her thighs, separating her pussy, exposing her clit to me, and I rub small circles in the sensitive flesh, loving when she gasps, a moan sneaking out of her mouth. I keep going, just for another minute. I was supposed to be teasing her, making her beg for it, but instead, here I am, getting my fill of her body right before the show starts.

I slide my fingers down, spreading her. She moves her legs apart for me, giving me better access to her cunt. I smile up at her, her eyes glued to me, her lip in between her teeth as she tries to hold back how badly she wants me to make her cum.

I get right outside of her entrance, my fingers seconds away from plunging inside, but I hold off, making her wait, just a moment, finding my self-restraint at last. She whimpers in the back of her throat, her hips thrusting, grinding against my hand, desperately trying to get me inside of her, but I just stare at my pretty wife, enjoying her right on the edge of pleasure.

"Stop teasing," she mutters, her voice a whine.

"I'm about to let a whole bunch of guys come in here and fuck you. I think a little bit of a tease is the least I could do," I say, swirling my fingers around her hole, my body itching to be inside of her. I feel at home when her cunt is wrapped around me, any part of my body, really. My fingers, my cock, my tongue. As long as I am inside of her, I am happy.

"As if you aren't just as desperate to watch me get fucked," she says, her voice turning cocky, like she knows she has me by the balls, and let's be honest here, she does. She knows me so well, too well sometimes, and that means she knows every single one of my tells. She knows when I want something, knows when I'm fucking desperate for it.

I lift up suddenly, removing my fingers from her cunt, not wanting to be the first one inside of her, not tonight. I'm always the first one she fucks, the only one she fucks, but tonight isn't about me. It's about my wife finding her pleasure and me enjoying the show.

"Why don't you sit up? I need to fasten your legs," I say with a smirk, giving her a light smack on the ass while she stares at me with her mouth wide. She really thought I was going to finger fuck her, really thought she might be able to cum even before this, but I'm not going to give in that easily. She is about to get more pleasure than she's ever had.

She nods, her eyes lighting on fire when she glances at the platform in front of her. There are steps to make it a little easier to get up, and she climbs on with ease, laying down, poking her legs through the plastic pieces. She slides through, giving me less and less of a view of her, but when I get to the other side, it's a fucking picture.

The other room is mostly bare, a few chairs surrounding the walls, a couch sitting on the far wall, but the main show is the platform jutting out from the wall, right at waist height, with my wife's cunt exposed to me, as she sits there with her knees up, waiting for me to chain her legs to the wall.

I walk over to her, thinking about what it is going to be like for these guys, these strangers to walk into this room and find my wife like this. I grab one of her legs, a small gasp sounding from the room beyond, and I think about the fact that she won't know when one of them is going to touch her, when one of them is going slide their cock inside of her, until they are already doing it, already fucking her tight cunt.

I wrap my hand around the ankle and lift, bringing her foot right in line with the straps, giving myself access to tie her legs up, giving her no way of getting out of this, unless she uses the safe word. The chain is almost like a belt. It allows me to make it as tight or as loose as I please, and then the leather is connected to a chain, which binds it to a wall. The straps are off to the side, forcing my wife to spread her legs, giving the best access to her pussy. She is going to be completely spread open for them when they walk into the room. Her cunt is going to be the first thing they see.

I do the same with her other leg, leaving her in front of me strapped to this contraption, completely at my mercy. I stare at her body, at her cunt, just for a moment, and then join her back in the room, closing the door behind me. My entire body is starting to vibrate with excitement, my entire being wanting to see her with another man's cock inside of her as soon as humanly possible.

"You ready?" I ask, looking down at her, her head in almost a perfect spot for my cock if she turns to the side, and I think that it must have been fate that I found her, found someone who is so willing, so horny that she wants this as much as I do.

Chapter 7

Kendall

The light turns green before I can answer, stealing both of our attention. We glance back at each other, once we have both processed what that means, and I smile excitedly, my body thrumming. I didn't think I would be this nervous, but my heart is beating out of my chest, my entire body radiating energy.

I hear the door open in the other room and voices start to invade my senses. I can hear them getting closer, hearing more than a few guys enter, and then I hear the door click shut, and I assume they are all inside, staring at my cunt. I'm completely exposed to them, my body literally on display, and I fidget with my hands, not knowing what to do with myself.

I can feel their gaze on me, a ton of eyes just taking my body in, and then, I hear a voice.

"Jesus Christ, look at that pretty pussy," one of them mutters, seemingly stepping closer. I expected to be turned on, expected to be dripping wet. What I didn't expect, though, was to be listening for every sound. Every footstep, every breath from the other side steals my attention, keeping me right on the edge.

"This is like a fucking wet dream," one guy mutters, their voices all seeming to mix together, my ears not able to pick out differences. This is so thrilling, having no idea how many guys are on the other side of this wall, how many guys are staring at the most intimate part of my body.

"Dude, I fucking know, right?" another guy comments. I bite my lip, waiting, waiting, waiting, desperate for them to touch me.

"So, who wants to go first?" someone asks, his voice cocky, almost degrading, like I am a ride at an amusement park, like I am more object than human and something about that makes me shiver with desire.

"Fuck, I got no problem going first," another guy says, a voice that I don't think I've heard yet. A couple of guys murmur, and then someone moves closer to me, close enough that

I can feel the heat of his body. I swear I hold my fucking breath, waiting for him to touch me, desperate for this to start.

"I bet this tight little cunt is gonna feel like heaven," he murmurs, barely loud enough for me to hear, and then he is touching me, his fingers trailing up my thighs, a shiver running through me at the contact. "God, you're a reactive one, huh?" he asks, and I whimper, the sound in my throat feeling completely foreign, but I feel like a different person, an animal in this moment. I feel less than human, more like a bundle of desire that just needs to be sated.

He's touching me, teasing me by just barely running his hands up and down my thighs, keeping me right on edge. I hold back another whimper, desperate to keep ahold of my dignity, at least for a bit longer.

It's so bizarre to be on the other side of a wall while someone is touching me. I've never been touched like this, never had one of my senses stripped away from me in this way. It makes every touch feel like more...and makes me even more sensitive. I feel every cell in my body, waiting for him, waiting to be pleasured by the stranger on the other side of this wall.

He finally, fucking finally, brings his fingers closer to my pussy, inching slowly, slowly, slowly, and I swear I'm two seconds away from begging, barely hanging onto my self-control, and then he touches me, his fingers running up and down my slit, still barely adding any pressure, but that feeling alone is enough to make my back arch, desire fucking coursing through me.

"He's touching your pussy, isn't he?" Nate asks, and I glance back up at him. I got lost there for a second, so consumed by the man on the other side of the wall that I didn't even think about the fact that my husband could see my every movement, my every reaction. I feel my cheeks heat, my face blooming red. He could tell, just based on my reactions, that a stranger is currently touching my pussy.

The stranger pushes a little harder, his fingers rubbing circles in my clit. In most situations, it would be mandatory to touch me before fucking me because I'd need to be prepped, but for this, I'm already soaking, so this is just torture, just an extra step until we get to the good part.

I try to hold back my moans and my reactions, my eyes now locked on my husband. It's almost embarrassing to be pleasured when he is right there. It feels like I'm doing something wrong, like I'm betraying him in this moment, even though I know rationally, I'm not. He wants this. He wants to see me get fucked just as much as I want to be fucked.

But then the stranger inserts a finger inside of me, and a guttural moan leaks out, my body not able to stop my reaction. He pumps his finger in and out of me, slowly at first, then picking up speed. It feels too good. My body is already too wound up. I have been thinking about this for so goddamn long, desperate for it, and now, I don't know how I'm going to keep myself from cumming, from orgasming right on this stranger's hand before he has even gotten a chance to fuck me.

"So, how does he feel inside of you?" Nate asks, looking down at me, his eyebrows raised in judgment, and I know he is just playing a part and just leaning into this kink. For some reason, his reaction is so fucking hot, like I'm not supposed to be turned on right now, like the reaction my body is having is one that I shouldn't be experiencing. Like it is against my will.

Jesus, this is wrong, this whole situation. It shouldn't be turning me on to think like this, to think about how bad I am being, that my husband is sitting here, watching me get fucked, and the idea that he doesn't want me to react, that he doesn't want to see my pleasure, almost like I'm keeping it a secret from him, what this stranger is doing to me on the other side of the wall, turns me on more, makes my pussy fucking drip around the stranger's finger.

The stranger takes his finger out, and I'm breathing heavily, my body wanting more, needing more, but part of me is relieved. I was so worried that I was going to cum, that my body wasn't going to be able to help itself. I am trying to hold back, trying not to show my husband how much I am enjoying this other man, but it's so fucking hard when it feels so goddamn good.

"God, she's fucking soaked," the stranger mutters, the other men around him making small comments and grunts of approval. I imagine them all over there, jerking their cocks while they watch another man, probably a stranger to them too, finger fuck me.

I wish I could be a fly on the wall and see into the other room, see how they are all reacting to me, all watching my body. I want to see the lust on all their faces, the expressions as they watch my desire drip off of this stranger's hand.

But half of the appeal of this is that I can't see a single thing.

I hear the clink of a belt buckle, and I imagine this stranger taking his cock out, leaving his pants on, just taking his dick out enough to fuck me, to use my little hole as he pleases. I'm right on the edge of my seat, literally holding my breath, trying to hear everything. I hear more movement. And I sense him moving closer to me, the heat of his body against the bare skin of my thighs.

And then, I feel the tip of his cock right at my entrance. He is right there, sliding through my cunt, rubbing himself all over me, getting the head of his dick wet. I bite my lip, trying to hold back a moan, trying to keep myself from reacting, but then he is slipping inside, going so fucking slow that it is torture. The head of his cock is inside of me, and I feel my back arch, my pussy aching to feel him inside of me completely.

I glance up at my husband as he stands in front of me, his eyes burning a fucking hole inside of me. He looks at me with lust, with a desire I have never seen before. I stare at him as this stranger slowly fucks me, sliding deep into me. I grunt as he bottoms out, his cock big, almost too big, even though I'm literally dripping all over myself.

"He's fucking you, isn't he?" Nate asks, staring down at me, his eyebrow raised. I nod at him, biting my lip, trying to keep from moaning.

"Jesus Christ, she's fucking tight,' the stranger mutters, pulling his cock from inside of me and then thrusting into me again. "Fuck, I'm going to cum way too quick," he whispers just loud enough for me to hear, for Nate to hear.

"Fuck, I think he likes that tight little hole," Nate mutters, bringing his hand down to my cheek, cupping my face, and then slapping lightly, his affection turning dirty quickly. "I knew they would love it, would love being inside of you. They are all going to be addicted after this. They will all fight me for another round with you, but you're not going to let them fuck you again, are you?" he says, his words causing literally goosebumps to spread over my arms. I try to think straight, try to come up with a reply, but I'm getting fucked by this stranger, and it's literally making my vision blur.

He isn't going slowly anymore. Instead, he is thrusting into me as he pleases, and that probably shouldn't turn me on. It feel dirty and nasty, but sitting here, being used as a sex toy for a man that isn't my husband, feels so fucking good, so fucking erotic.

"Fuck," the stranger moans, and I feel my back start to arch. His hand comes down on my clit, rubbing small circles, and I can't fucking take it. It's too fucking good. He is so deep, fucking into me with reckless abandon, and my husband is standing over me, watching as pleasure takes over my face, and now, this stranger is trying to get me to cum.

"You going to cum for him?" my husband asks, leaning down so our faces are closer together. His breath is on my neck as he whispers in my ear. I want him to touch me, to use me too, but he just stands over me, my body shaking with desire. "Are you about to cum for another man?" he asks, and I feel myself fill with embarrassment and shame that I am this close already for someone other than him. The shame shouldn't make my pussy tense up, shouldn't bring me closer to the orgasm I'm trying to run away from, but it does.

Feeling like a slut, a slut who can't help but cum on another man's cock, is so fucking hot it's unholy.

"You better not cum for him, Kendall," he says, warning in his tone. I know he is loving this. His eyes are alive with desire, his entire body thrumming with need, but we are playing a game. That's what this entire situation is, a scene for us to get off, and he is playing it too fucking well for me to last as long as I thought I could.

"I won't," I say, my voice tight. I'm barely hanging on as is, barely keeping myself from falling off of the edge. It's all just too much, too much pleasure, too much desire running through me. Nate runs one of his hands down my torso, taking my tit in his hand, and then he squeezes my nipple, making this even harder.

"Really?" he asks, looking at me like he knows how close I am, how I'm about to cum for another man.

"Guys, she is so fucking tight right now, holy fuck," the stranger says, a groan coming out, his desire for me dripping from his voice. "I think she's going to cum," he says, and a few guys grunt in approval, moans leaking from the crowd, their cocks probably out as they watch their fellow stranger fuck me.

"Fuck," I moan, my entire body starting to vibrate. I try to pull my legs closer together, try to push off the pleasure, but I'm strapped down, unable to move my legs. I try to close my knees together, but the stranger on the other side just pushes them back, fucking into me, his cock hitting so fucking deep it is making me squirm.

"Oh, are you going to cum?" Nate asks, stealing my attention back. It's like I can't focus on anything. My body is right on the edge. As they both demand my attention, it makes it harder and harder to keep from cumming, to keep my body from responding the way it so desperately wants to.

"No, no," I reply, my back arching, my tits moving with each thrust that the stranger makes into my body. "I promise. I won't," I say, my voice a literal cry, my body completely doing the opposite of what I need it to do. I'm so fucking turned on, this entire situation being such a fucking shock to the system that my body can't hold back.

"Wait, wait, wait," I say, trying to get the stranger to stop playing with my clit, trying to get him to give me a second to rest, but he doesn't. He just goes harder.

"What? You don't want to cum for me while your husband is right there?" he asks, a laugh in his voice, and he just keeps going, giving me not a fucking second to rest, and then, I'm fucking cumming, my entire body tensing under the pleasure.

I moan so fucking loudly, my back arching, my cunt pulsing around his cock, but he doesn't stop. He just fucks me harder, riding me through my orgasm, his fingers on my clit just going faster, harder, until it is too much.

I start to come down, my vision literally blurry as I bring myself back to earth. My body is sweaty and sore from how long I was tensing. I do my best to catch my breath, heaving in and out as Nate plays with one of my tits, leaning over me and holding my head in his hand, staring at me, his face close.

"I thought you said you weren't going to cum," he says sadly, his voice dripping with disappointment. I stare at him, trying like hell to catch my breath, my mind trying to come back into this moment.

"I'm sorry," I say desperately, reaching for him. "I'm sorry, I couldn't stop it," I say, trying to get him to understand, but he just pulls away, tsks, and then says something I am not expecting.

"If she is going to act like a whore, treat her like one. Why don't you guys fill her up with your cum and then see how she likes it," he says, loud enough for the group outside to hear, and my eyes widen. We hadn't discussed if they would cum inside. I'm on birth control, and everyone got tested before this. That was a must to make sure this was as safe as possible, but I just figured they would cum on me or something.

"You know what to say if you don't want that to happen," he says, leaning closer to me, waiting for me to say the safe word, waiting to see if I don't want this.

The thing is, though, I do. I want it so desperately. I was so excited to be fucked by these guys, and I didn't even think about where they would cum, where their desire would land when it was all said and finished. I want their cum. I want to be filled up like a used sex toy, want to be used until they are all done with me. I want to make a fucking mess on the floor with all of their seed, the evidence of what happened here, right between my legs.

"That's what I thought," he says. "I knew a slut like you would want their cum," he says, shaking his head like he can't believe me. God, his disappointment in me is so fucking hot like he can't believe he married such a fucking slut wife.

"Holy fuck," the stranger mutters, his thrusting turning faster, turning more erratic, his entire body thrumming with desire, and then he is groaning, cumming inside of me, just like my husband told him to, and I'm tightening around him, taking his cum, desperate for it to stay inside of me for as long as possible.

"Did he just cum inside of my wife?" Nate whispers, looking down at me. I stare up at him, my eyes fucking wide, and I nod slowly, waiting for his backlash. This should not be hot, should not be making my pussy clench around nothing as the stranger removes his cock from me, telling someone else to step up and take their turn.

Another man steps up, the sounds of his footsteps muffled as he comes closer to me, and then his belt buckle is clinking together, the telltale sign that I'm about to get fucked again, and I stare at my husband as he watches me, his eyes burning with passion.

"If you're going to act like such a fucking slut, you can at least get me off while I watch you fuck other men," my husband says, and then he removes his pants, his cock out before I have a second to react, and then, as if in fucking sync,

I'm being fucked by my two men: my husband in my mouth and a stranger into my pussy.

I moan around my husband's cock, my body sucking in both of them, desire running through me. This is too much, even for me. I'm so fucking wet, so fucking horny, and this situation is only getting more fucking intense.

"Fuck, she's so fucking warm and wet," the new stranger says, his cock thrusting in and out of me slowly at first, getting us both used to it. "Jesus Christ, I don't know how you lasted so fucking long man. She feels too fucking good," he says, groaning. He grabs my legs, using them to steady himself, and then he slides into me again, his cock not as long as the last guy but thicker, forcing me to stretch around him. I moan around my husband's cock again, my hands grabbing onto the edges of the table, desperate not to cum again, desperate to keep my desire at bay. "Fuck, you like that I'm fucking his cum deeper inside of you?" the stranger asks, and that visual, the idea that he is thrusting another random guy's cum all the way to my womb, makes my fucking back arch, giving my husband a better angle to stuff his cock deeper, until I'm fucking gagging.

"Fuck, take this cock into the back of your throat. If all these other guys are going to get to fuck you, I'm going to use your tight little throat too," my husband groans, thrusting his cock deeper, hitting the back of my throat. Then he's pushing, forcing me to take as much as humanly fucking possible, while this stranger is fucking me ruthlessly.

"Dude, play with her clit. You have to feel how fucking tight she is when she cums," the last stranger says, his voice a little farther back. I imagine him at the edge, jerking his cock now, enjoying the show after getting his fill of me.

"Fuck, I'm already so close," the stranger fucking me groans, pushing deeper, deeper, using my cunt like a fleshlight.

"She is so fucking reactive dude. It won't take much. She's a fucking whore," the other stranger reminds him, and I swear their conversion is turning me on even more. Hearing these guys talk about me like this, talk about my body as if I'm not even here, is doing things to me that I wasn't fucking ready for.

The guy fucking me starts playing with my clit, per the other guy's instructions, and I swear I'm already close to cumming again. Usually, it isn't this easy for me to reach orgasm. Usually, it takes a lot longer to get there, but this, this situation is hitting every one of my senses, making it impossible to last.

"Fuck, you hear them talking about you? Like you aren't even fucking here," Nate mutters, pulling his cock out, leaving just the tip in my mouth. I swirl my tongue around it, doing my best to please him too, wanting his cum in my mouth, wanting cum in every single hole that I have. "Fuck, you want my cum too? I swear, you could get fucked by every cock on this earth, and it wouldn't be enough for your slutty holes," he says, thrusting his cock deep again. He brings his hands down to my tits, playing with my nipples until I whimper, this assault on my body being too fucking much.

I know I shouldn't be this close to cumming again, shouldn't cum for every single one of these guys, at the least in the game me and Nate are playing, but fuck, they are making my body fucking desperate for more. I'm already trying to grind against the guy fucking me, needing him deeper, harder. I want more and more and more and more, but if I have any fucking more, I'm going to cum so fucking hard, and every man in this room is going to know what a whore I am.

But, I'm just too cock hungry to resist.

Chapter 8

Nate

I swear to fucking god, I knew this was going to be hot. I just didn't think my cock was going to ache to fill my wife full of cum at every goddam second. Watching her cum on another man's cock, watching her be pleasured by someone else, was supposed to be hot, but I didn't realize it was going to be fucking addicting.

Watching my wife choke down my dick, taking it deep enough that I can see exactly where it is in her throat, while another guy gets her closer and closer to another orgasm, feels like an out-of-body experience.

She is doing her best to hold off, playing the shame and humiliation game that we are playing, but I know she is already close, moments away from orgasm. If she let herself go, she would be cumming hard already, but she is resisting, trying to keep from seeing me be disappointed in her again, but I think she gets off on my disappointment.

She whines around my cock, probably trying to beg one of us to stop, because she's too close, but I don't listen. I just keep thrusting, playing with her nipples in my hands, exactly the way I know she likes, trying like hell to drive her closer to the edge.

I hear the wet slaps of her skin against the guy who is fucking her, the sound filling both of the rooms, and I swear I could get off on it. I'm sure the sight of my wife getting fucked is to die for, and suddenly I wish I was recording that room, just so I could see how all of them react when they get inside of my tight, wet wife and feel that she is fucking heaven.

Her cunt is my religion, and after tonight, it's going to be theirs too. They just don't get to take it home and worship it after blowing their loads inside of her.

"Fuck, I can feel how fucking close she is," the guy behind the wall says, his voice hoarse, and I can tell he is close too. God, we are all right on the edge of cumming, holding back. I need her to cum first, need her to cum with another guy's dick in her pussy and my cock in her throat.

She tries to shake her head, barely able to move with my cock so fucking deep, and I stare down at her, communicating with my eyes. I raise an eyebrow, thrusting in and out, and she shakes her head again, trying to tell me that she isn't going to cum, but the longer we go, the longer I stare at her while she gets fucked by another man, the harder it is for her to hang on.

Her eyes close, her back arching off the platform, and then she is moaning around my cock, her body doing what she can't. She is orgasming, for the both of us, for all the men in that room who are enjoying watching my wife.

I thrust deeper, watching her throat bulge, watching her start to come down from her orgasm, and then, I blow my load inside of her throat, making her choke on it. I thrust while I cum, filling up her mouth with my cum, making her take every fucking drop. When I finally pull out, she sputters, desperate for air, my cum being coughed out, and she tries to breathe, making a mess all over her face.

I wanted her to swallow, wanted to know that my load was deep inside of her stomach, but this works too. I take my wet cock and drag it across her face, spreading my seed around, letting it soak into her skin.

And then, like dominos, the guy fucking her groans too, cumming deep inside of my wife, filling her from both ends.

RHIANNA BURWELL

God, the sight is so fucking good, my wife with my load on her face, taking another man's cum while he pounds into her, fucking her like he is trying to find God.

Chapter 9

Kendall

Holy shit.

This is too good, too much for me. I'm fucking addicted. I have never came like this, never experienced something so nasty, so disgusting, so fucking erotic. This isn't supposed to happen to normal people because it melts their brains. I literally think that's happening to me. My brain is melted as I come down from my second orgasm, cum all over my face, thankfully missing my eyes, as I get filled to the brim with my second load from a stranger.

"Jesus Christ," the stranger groans, shooting the rest of his load inside of me, his hands gripping my thighs for support and then he's pulling out, my purpose done, his desire unloaded inside of me. "She gets so fucking tight when she comes dude. You were right," he says, his voice moving away.

"Look at you, covered in cum, just like you wanted," Nate mutters, looking down at me, his cock still hard, his cum coating my skin. "You look just like the whore we know you are," he says, a small smile taking over. I can see his love for me, right in his gaze, and it comforts me. It reminds me that this is something we are doing together, something that is only happening because of the trust between us.

"Fuck, I'm going next," I hear another guy mutter from the other side of the wall, his body moving closer, his footsteps giving me an inkling of where he is. There is a second or two of hesitation, and then, he slaps my pussy lips with his cock, hitting my clit, and making me gasp. "Oh, I think she likes that, boys," he says, his voice echoing all around me. A few guys chuckle, enjoying the show, and god, the idea of them all over there, just getting off on me is so fucking hot. They are all lusting after me, enjoying my body. It's driving me fucking crazy.

"I think they are enjoying my little toy," Nate whispers, just loud enough for me to hear, his cock still rubbing across my face. I glance up at him, my tits begging to be touched, my body so ready for more pleasure, as if it hasn't had enough already. God, maybe I am the whore they say I am. Maybe I am so fucking horny that my cunt can't even be satisfied after being fucked by two different cocks.

"God, I bet you wish you could see this. Your pussy is leaking cum right now all over the place," The stranger mutters, his cock sliding through my slit, making me buck and moan, wanting him to dip inside so fucking badly, but not wanting to expose that I'm still a horny fucking mess.

He slaps my clit with his cock again, and I gasp again. The sounds coming out of me are unholy as he keeps doing it, completely over-sensitizing me in the best fucking way. "God, you are so fucking reactive it should be illegal," he groans, then slides his cock inside of me, thrusting so fucking deep, giving me everything he has right off the bat.

My back arches as I get used to his size, as my pussy sucks him deeper, wanting more and more and more.

"You're ruining them all, Kendall. They are going to think about this night, think about this tight fucking cunt until they die, wishing for more. They are never going to be satisfied after this," Nate groans, putting his dick against my lips, and pushing, silently telling me to open up.

I do, sticking my tongue out for him, and he slaps his cock against it, just like the stranger was doing to me, and I whine.

I'm so turned on, so overcome with pleasure that I don't even know what to do with myself.

I have never felt this horny, never felt like I couldn't be satisfied, but that's how I feel, like my skin is going to melt off if I don't cum again like my heart will simply stop beating if there isn't a cock inside of me.

"Does his cock feel good inside of you?" my husband asks, looking down at me with shame in his gaze. He slides his cock inside of my mouth, only giving me the tip, and I groan, wanting more, wanting the whole thing, deep. I want to be fucked from both ends, feeling so much that I am just a ball of pleasure for their taking.

I nod my head, answering his question, and he brings his fingers down on the root of his dick, sliding it deep into my throat. "I guess my slutty wife likes to be fucked by other guys," he says, as I start to gag, my throat only being able to take so much, but he goes another inch, not giving me a second to catch my breath until he is my throat, thrusting in and out like he is jerking off with my body as his sex toy.

All the while, the new stranger is fucking me, giving me no mercy, my pussy already drenching, dripping with cum, if his assessment is correct. I've already been fucked twice, so I don't need any prep, and he isn't going to give me any.

He is thrusting quickly, using me, and it's so fucking good. I moan around Nate's cock, loving the feeling of both of them inside of me. I feel my pleasure start to build, my third orgasm of the night starting to take root inside of my spine, but the stranger is going too fast, using my body like his only aim is to cum quickly, to shoot me with as much of his cum as he can. And before I know it, he is groaning, pounding his fist on the wall in front of me, the wall connecting us, and his orgasm takes him over, unholy sounds escaping his mouth.

"Fuck, I couldn't fucking last. She's so goddamn tight, guys. I don't know how you did it," he says to the other men in the room. He pulls out, and I hate the feeling of emptiness that overtakes me. I want to be filled again, want another man inside of me directly after the last. I should be upset that he didn't make me cum, but god, it just adds to the idea that I'm being used. He didn't even care if I came. He just fucked into my body like it was his for the taking.

I hear another man step up, but my ears are ringing. Nate fucking my throat so hard that he is stealing every ounce of my focus.

"That's right. Look at me. Pay attention to your husband," he says, while another man slips inside of me, his cock hitting me deep. I groan against Nate's cock, and he moans, enjoying the vibration.

The new stranger fucking me instantly starts playing with my clit.

"Don't worry baby, I'll make sure you cum," he says, my body starting to fucking shut down with how much pleasure is coursing through me right now.

Like I said, I think this is fucking breaking me. I think after we are done, after all the guys on the other side of the wall have had their way with me, I'm going to be a shell of the person I was, only a vessel for this pleasure. I'm going to be an addict, needing more and more and more, and I don't know if I'm ever going to get enough.

Chapter 10

Kendall

The stranger fucking me isn't giving me a second to breathe. Actually, my husband isn't giving me a second to breathe either, literally. His cock is so deep in my throat, cutting off my oxygen, but he doesn't stop, doesn't act like he cares about me, only cares about seeking his pleasure inside of me.

The stranger, though, is rubbing my clit, forcing me closer and closer to the edge of another orgasm, of more pleasure, even though I have already been completely overloaded in the best way possible.

"Fuck, I can feel how much you like this," the stranger groans, feeling me tense up. He's fucking me deep, grinding against me with each stroke, doing things to me that I didn't even know were possible. I didn't realize I could feel like this, this soaked with cum, with desire, with need.

"Fuck, baby, you going to cum for him? Show him how fucking tight you get when that pussy cums?" Nate says, looking down at me with his cock deep in my throat. The power he has is fucking insane. He is so goddamn attractive, so hot in this moment, and I can't take my eyes away. I want to stare at him while he fucks my throat, while he finds pleasure in my tight holes, until he cums, until he unloads inside of me, forcing me to take it like the slut he knows I am.

He pulls out, giving me just a second to breathe, and I gasp for breath, drool spilling out of my mouth, a line of spit connecting his cock to my mouth. His hand extends closer to me, smearing the spit, the cum, all over my fucking face, blending it all together until it's a fucking mess, my face wet with what has happened here. It feels so dirty, like he is treating me exactly as I deserve, as someone who needs pleasure like this, who needs to be treated like such a whore.

The stranger is still fucking me, his thrusts so fucking hard they are starting to shake the wall, and I'm not sure how much longer I can take. My pussy is probably dripping all over the floor, my desire mixing with the cum. I'm just a fucking mess of fluids, too cock hungry to even care in this moment.

"Fuuuck, you are getting so fucking tight," the stranger mutters, his thrusts only getting harder, faster, and I feel as though I have stopped processing anything.

I know Nate starts fucking my throat again, the force of his thrusts hitting the back of my throat hard enough that they start to hurt. I know the stranger is fucking me hard, forcing my cunt to take more than it should, but I'm loving every second of it. I know I am seconds away from cumming, my desire too fucking high, too much to handle all of this, but I can't even think anymore, can't breathe because I'm too wound up.

And then I'm cumming, my back arching so fucking high I swear I'm going to break in half, and I feel Nate shoot his load inside of my mouth at the height of pleasure, the salty taste of his cum only making me soar a little higher. I can feel that my orgasm sends the stranger over the edge too, but I'm too trapped, my brain a pile of mush, to process what the fuck is happening.

I come back too, breathing heavy, more drool spilling out of my mouth, mixed with Nate's cum, and he is breathing heavily too, standing over me like he just saw god, and I think I may have too.

Chapter 11

Nate

I stare down at my wife, cum and spit all over her face, her chest moving so quickly that I'm slightly worried she isn't getting enough air, and I swear to God, she has never looked better than she does right now. I'm so in love with her, so fucking amazed by her and what she has added to my life, what she has been willing to give me. I think I'm the luckiest fucking guy on earth, that now, I get to care for her, get to take her home and make sure that she is okay, make sure that all of her needs are met.

She is exhausted. I can see it on her face. Her eyes are starting to droop, and she is staring at the ceiling, trying to catch her breath, trying to come back down to earth. I hear the guys leave, all four of them. I found them on dating websites, made them get tested, made other women vouch for them, made sure they were safe if they were going to be touching my wife, and briefed them on what was going to be happening. I also told them, that once they were all done, they needed to go home. It's my turn to step in now.

I hear the door click in the other room, but I stay put, wanting to be close to my wife, wanting to hold her in my arms, but I need to do a few things first.

"You okay?" I ask, staring down at her, love in my gaze. I'm sure I look like those people in cartoons when their eyes shoot out of their heads with hearts. That's how I feel, so fucking in love it goddamn hurts. I tuck my cock back in my pants, righting myself while I'm at it, knowing she is going to need a few minutes before she is ready to move, if she can move at all, if her muscles aren't too tense, too sore after the pounded she just got.

"Holy fuck," she says, still breathing hard. She wipes some of the spit from her chin, but there is so much, such a sticky mess, that it doesn't even make a dent in cleaning her up. "Yeah, I'm okay. That was fucking intense," she says, looking back at the ceiling, her chest moving with each breath, her tits jiggling.

I grab my bag, the one I brought in with me, the one she didn't think twice about, and grab the wipes from inside, zipping it closed after. I go to her, pulling a few wipes out, and clean her face, taking every remnant of my cum, of her spit, and wiping it away.

She stares up at me as I do this, and I swear this moment, this action right here, feels more intimate than what we just did. That was nasty, disgusting, a way for both of us to get our rocks off, have good orgasms, but this? This is love, pure and unbothered. I love watching her in this moment, her face bare, her hair a fucking mess. She is exactly who I married, the person who I see every morning, and who I love more than anyone else.

This is the person I would die for, the person who steals my breath every goddamn day, and this moment is no different.

"Are you okay?" she asks, grabbing my hand, her head tilting, just barely, like she isn't sure of what my answer is going to be. I stare down at her, just for a second, loving the sincerity on her face.

"That was the hottest thing I've ever seen. I think I may be ruined forever, but yeah, I'm okay," I say with a smile, and she smiles, too. Her face breaks out into a grin that takes every ounce of oxygen in the room.

"That's how I feel, too," she says, laughing lightly. The intensity of the moment shatters, and now we are just two people, so hopelessly in love, so desperate to be around another, who just had the best orgasms of their lives.

"Let me get you unhooked," I say, bringing my hand to her face, needing to feel her for just a moment before I walk away. She leans into my touch, seeming to need it, seeming to want it. I pull away, walk out the door, and see the fucking mess that is in the other room.

My wife's legs are there, against a wall, a pile of cum still leaking out of her, cum on the platform below her ass, and a pile on the ground, a fucking puddle of cum on the floor under her. It probably shouldn't make me want a round with her, shouldn't make my cock stiffen in my pants, but it does. The sight of her being fucking used like this is so goddamn hot.

But right now, no matter how badly I want to be inside of her, I know I need to take care of her now, need to show her how loved and appreciated she is. I can make love to her later, and that's what it would be. This was sex, dirty, nasty sex, but when I get my hands on her later, after I get her a bath and a meal, I'm going to take my time, find pleasure in her body, until both of us are right on the edge, both of us being vulnerable with each other in a way that none of these other guys will get to experience.

Only me, her husband.

I walk toward her, being mindful not to step in the puddle of cum, and softly place my hand on her leg, letting her know I'm there. She sucks in a breath and then relaxes against me. It takes me no time at all to get her unfastened, and then her legs are free, and she is scooting away from me, into a sitting position.

I walk back into the room, find her sitting there, stretching her legs, and rotating her ankles. I'm sure she is sore after sitting there tied up for so long. She smiles at me, her face so fucking cute right now, probably a word that doesn't make sense after what I saw her do, but god, it's how I feel.

"I feel like I just ran a marathon," she says with a smile, stretching her other leg, cum still running from inside of her, leaking onto the table. I grab the wipes again, moving toward her with one in my hand. She tries to stop me, tries to grab my hand and do it herself, but I don't let go. I won't allow her to do this herself, not this part.

"Let me," I say softly, seriousness in my gaze. This is my job to take care of the woman that I love, to see her through the end of this. She needs to be taken care of now and shown all the love in the world.

"Thank you," she says softly, her voice quavering. I wipe softly through her pussy, cleaning her up, cleaning over her ass, cleaning every last drop of cum on her skin until she is clean and emotional. I look at her, wondering what more she needs, what more I can give her to make her feel better because that's all I want. "I'm sorry. This was so much fun. It was just intense. I don't know why I'm feeling like this," she says, her voice starting to blubber, tears filling her eyes.

I pull her closer to me, her skin against mine, needing her near me. "I know. It's okay. It was a lot. It makes sense that you will have feelings come up," I say softly, and she nods into me. "Let's get you home. I'll run you a bath, feed you, and then we can get some sleep," I say, stroking her hair, trying my best to comfort her.

"Okay," she says lightly while nodding. I help her get dressed slowly. Her body is sore as hell, but I love it. I enjoy being the person here for the aftermath, being the person who gets to take her home and care for her after all of this. She apologizes a few times during the process, but I don't think she understands that this is the best part for me, feeling close to her, feeling like she is mine and I am hers. I may have just watched a whole bunch of guys fuck her, but we still belong to each other, and that's what I care about.

She is sitting on the platform, on one of the few bare spots that aren't sticky, and she stares at me while I gather our things. "Nate?" she asks, her voice low.

I look toward her and hum in answer. "Hmm?"

"Are we going to come back here?" she asks, her voice vulnerable. I turn toward her, needing to see her face. I need to see her reactions if we are going to talk about this.

"Do you want to come back here?" I ask, and she nods instantly, giving me her answer. "Then, of course, we will. You aren't the only one who had a good time, baby," I say and stroke my hand down her cheek again. She smiles at me, that smile that I know means she's thinking about it, thinking about what happened in this room.

"I love you," she says, standing up, her feet wobbly. I go to help her, but she pushes me away, intent on walking on her own.

"I love you too, baby," I say with a smile, ignoring her and grabbing her hand, needing the contact. I think, somehow, we are leaving this room stronger than when we entered.

Chapter 12

Kendall

I think the coffee tastes better this morning, in the aftermath of what happened last night. It feels like the world around me has changed, has become a little bit brighter, like it has opened up in front of me, giving me a world of possibilities.

Or maybe... I've changed. Maybe I just became a different person last night, sitting on that wooden platform, getting fucked by different men while my husband was right there. Maybe it changed me, in a way I never expected but welcome all the same.

"What are you smiling about?" Nate asks, sitting across from me, his eyes lit up too, like something has been awoken inside of him, like he may be a different person just like I am.

He stares at me, love in his gaze, adoration coating me, and I feel myself swell with love.

"This is good coffee," I say, a smile on my face, almost permanently.

"I didn't do anything different," he says with a light laugh, probably seeing through me. My husband always seems to, always knows what I'm thinking before I have a chance to tell him.

"Maybe I'm different," I mutter, looking up at him, vulnerability in my gaze. Is it too soon to talk about this, too soon to rehash the events of last night, too soon to talk about doing it again? I don't know the answer, and usually that would be anxiety-inducing, would make nerves crawl under my skin and take root there, but instead, I feel safe enough to figure it out, to ask my husband what he wants, what he needs.

After last night, I know he will stick by me, through anything, will listen to any want, any need I have, and give it thought. After last night, I'm realizing my husband is more on the same page as me.

"Is that a good thing?" Nate asks, staring at me, trying to read me, and I let him. I feel closer to him, like I can trust him with anything, any part of me. I want him to see it all, want him to know me inside and out.

"Yeah, I think so," I say, the smile not leaving my mouth, no matter how hard I try. "What about you? Do you feel different?" I ask, already seeing a difference in him, seeing a light that wasn't there before, a comfort with me, that we haven't had in our relationship, but I want to know how he feels, what to know if he is experiencing a change, or if this is one-sided.

"I didn't really think it would be possible to fall in love with you anymore, but I think I did," Nate says, looking at me like he wants to kiss me, like he wants a round with me, like he wants to make love to me and then fuck me until we both have our fill.

"So, you're okay then? With everything that happened last night?" I ask, mostly knowing the answer, but wanting to hear him say it. My biggest fear with doing this, with moving forward with last night, was that it would change us, would change his opinion of me. I never wanted him to think differently of me, for our relationship to change, and I just need to know, that we are still solid, that we are okay after everything that happened, because that is my biggest concern.

"Kendall... I can't stop replaying it in my head, thinking about it over and over again, how you looked when you came on another guy's dick," he says, rubbing his jaw, his words forcing desire to run through me, forcing my legs to feel weak, forcing me to want more from him, to want another round. "I think it was the hottest thing I've ever fucking seen. I'm more worried about when we are going to do it again," he says, and I stare at him, waiting for him to take those words back.

We talked last night, about it happening again, about us coming back, but I knew it needed a more in-depth conversation, needing a sit-down talk. I wanted to make sure we were on the same page before we agreed to go again, but here we are, with my pussy already clenching around nothing, wishing we would find our way back to that room, so we could do it all over again. And here he is, seemingly feeling the same way.

"Does that mean you want to go back?" I ask, breathy, my desire sitting on my face, in my voice. I know he can tell, because his eyebrow raises, just barely, his tongue peaking out to wet his lip. He looks at me like he has sex on the brain, and so do I.

He moves slowly, watching me with every inch, moving to the floor, onto his knees in front of me, only a few feet away, but he moves closer, looking up at me with those goddamn sex eyes, and I'm putty in my chair before he's even touching me.

"Do you want to go back?" he asks, looking up at me, his body closer now, in front of me. He spreads my legs open, my shorts barely covering me. I let him move my body, inching myself down to give him better access to my pussy, needing his touch, needing something, anything.

"Yes," I say, desperate. I want to go back, so fucking badly. I thought last night would make it better, would curve this desire inside of me, but it has only made it worse, only made my addition grow, and now I want more.

"Well, I give my wife whatever she needs, don't I?" he asks, bringing my mouth down on my leg, right on my inner thigh, kissing my skin, the heat of his mouth addicting.

"Yes," I say, barely containing a moan. He's barely even touching me and already, I'm so filled with desire it is all-consuming.

"Then, I'll make sure you get fucked on that table again," he says, instantly bringing his mouth back down on my leg, kissing up, up, up, driving me fucking wild with how slow he is going. "But for now, this pussy is mine," he says, looking up at me to confirm, to give him control.

All I can do is nod, not trusting my voice, my desire too high.

"Do you think I'll be able to taste their cum inside of you still?" he asks, moving my shorts to the side, my mouth coming down on my clit suddenly, and my back is arching, trying desperately to get closer to him, to get more friction, and he lets me, pushes his mouth against my cunt and licks, his tongue lapping at me, desperate for more.

He slips his finger inside of me, with the promise of what is to come, of the next time I'm going to be strapped to that table, and I swear to fucking God, my life could not get any better than this.

Books By This Author

Done Right (She Teaches Him #1):

What happens when Emma, who just wants to be done right, meets Finn, who doesn't know what he's doing?

Taught Right (She Teaches Him #2):

What happens when Joey, who just wants to be taught right, hires Ava, who knows exactly how to teach him?

F*cked Right (She Teaches Him #3):

What happens when Jace, who has never done this before, gets f*cked right by Callie, who knows exactly what she's doing?

Called Right (She Teaches Him #4):

Avery doesn't want a relationship, Reid does. So what happens when they decide to try out a vacation fling... over the phone?

Greedy:

What happens when the best kind of revenge, is fucking your ex-boyfriend's business rival?

White Christmas:

Their parents may be best friends, but Autumn and Theo have been enemies since birth. So what happens when they get snowed in at a hotel... and there's only one bed?

About The Author

Rhianna Burwell is an Amazon best seller in erotica. Author of the Before series and the She Teaches Him series, available on Kindle Unlimited, she takes pride in writing spicy, realistic, and deeply satisfying romance and erotica. Rhianna currently resides in Minnesota, where—when she's not writing erotica hot enough to melt all the winter snows—she enjoys curling up with her cat, avidly watching Grey's Anatomy, and reading—her current fav is alien romance. Rhianna loves to hear from readers, who can connect with via any of her social media links.

Instagram: @rhiannaburwellauthor
Tiktok: @rhiannaburwellauthor

Milton Keynes UK
Ingram Content Group UK Ltd.
UKHW021020290724
446271UK00015B/765